PLAYDATES RULE!

Rob McClurkan

BLOOMSBURY

NEW YORK LONDON OXFORD NEW DELHI SYDNEY

First published in the United States of America in November 2017
by Bloomsbury Children's Books
www.bloomsbury.com

Bloomsbury is a registered trademark of Bloomsbury Publishing Plc

For information about permission to reproduce selections from this book, write to
Permissions, Bloomsbury Children's Books, 1385 Broadway, New York, New York 10018
Bloomsbury books may be purchased for business or promotional use. For information on bulk purchases please contact
Macmillan Corporate and Premium Sales Department at specialmarkets@macmillan.com

Library of Congress Cataloging-in-Publication Data
available upon request
ISBN 978-1-68119-369-4 (hardcover) · ISBN 978-1-68119-370-0 (e-book) · ISBN 978-1-68119-711-1 (e-PDF)

Art created with Adobe Photoshop
Typeset in Bernhard Gothic
Lettering by Rob McClurkan
Book design by Heather Palisi
Printed in China by Leo Paper Products, Heshan, Guangdong
1 3 5 7 9 10 8 6 4 2

For my mom,
thanks for the playdates . . .
sorry about the sofa

I invited my best friend, Finley, over for our first playdate.

My parents were super excited to meet him.

We went to my room, where we planned our adventures. It was going to be the best day ever!

First, Finley gave me a piggyback ride.

That's when we heard playdate rule #1:

Then, Finley showed me how to make trumpet sounds.

That's when Dad told us playdate rule #2.

Only use inside voices. You can run around and make all the noise you want outside.

So we did! Until Mom shouted out playdate rule #3.

Finley and I found out playdates sure do have lots of rules, like . . .

#4. Don't ride your dad's bike.

#5. Don't help water your mom's plants.

#6. Don't dance in the tree house.

But then, I discovered Finley had never been on a trampoline . . .

BOING!

This was turning out to be a way cooler playdate than we had planned.

Finley felt terrible about the hole in the roof.
"It's okay," I said. "My dad loves fixing things!"
That made Finley smile.

Finally, it was time for Finley to go home.

Everyone was sad to see him go . . .